Mrs. Noah's Doves

For Peter Tacy, who would
build me an ark, if I asked —J.Y.

To children who love animals —A.M.

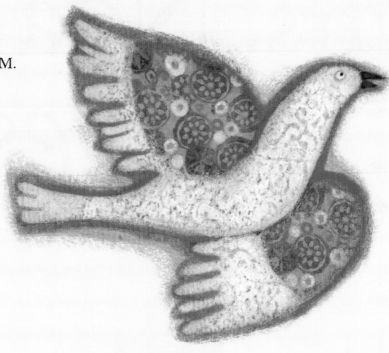

KAR-BEN PUBLISHING®
An imprint of Lerner Publishing Group, Inc.
241 First Avenue North
Minneapolis, MN 55401 USA

Website address: www.karben.com

Main body text set in Perpetua Regular.
Typeface provided by Monotype Typography.

Library of Congress Cataloging-in-Publication Data

Names: Yolen, Jane, author. | Massari, Alida, illustrator.
Title: Mrs. Noah's doves / Jane Yolen ; illustrated by Alida Massari.
Description: Minneapolis, MN : Kar-Ben Publishing , [2022] | Audience: Ages 5–9. | Audience: Grades 2–3. |
    Summary: Mrs. Noah nurses injured birds and brings them on board the ark when the heavy rains come, saving a
    special mission for the doves.
Identifiers: LCCN 2021014668 (print) | LCCN 2021014669 (ebook) | ISBN 9781728424262 | ISBN 9781728427935
    (paperback) | ISBN 9781728444178 (ebook)
Subjects: CYAC: Birds—Fiction. | Pigeons—Fiction. | Noah's ark—Fiction.
Classification: LCC PZ7.Y78 Mr 2022 (print) | LCC PZ7.Y78 (ebook) | DDC [E]—dc23

LC record available at https://lccn.loc.gov/2021014668
LC ebook record available at https://lccn.loc.gov/2021014669

Manufactured in the United States of America
1-49296-49412-6/9/2021

Mrs. Noah's Doves

Jane Yolen

Illustrations by Alida Massari

Before there was rain,
Mrs. Noah kept injured birds.
She kept ravens and robins,
eagles and eiders,
cockatoos and crows.
But her favorites were the doves.
They reminded her of her grandmother
cooing over the newest grandchild
or, at night, bending over to pray
in her soft, gray clothing.

She kept the sickest birds in cages.
Some of the cages were the gold of the sun.
Some were the silver of the moon.
But most cages were the blue of the sky
so that the birds would be comfortable
and unafraid until it was time to fly free.

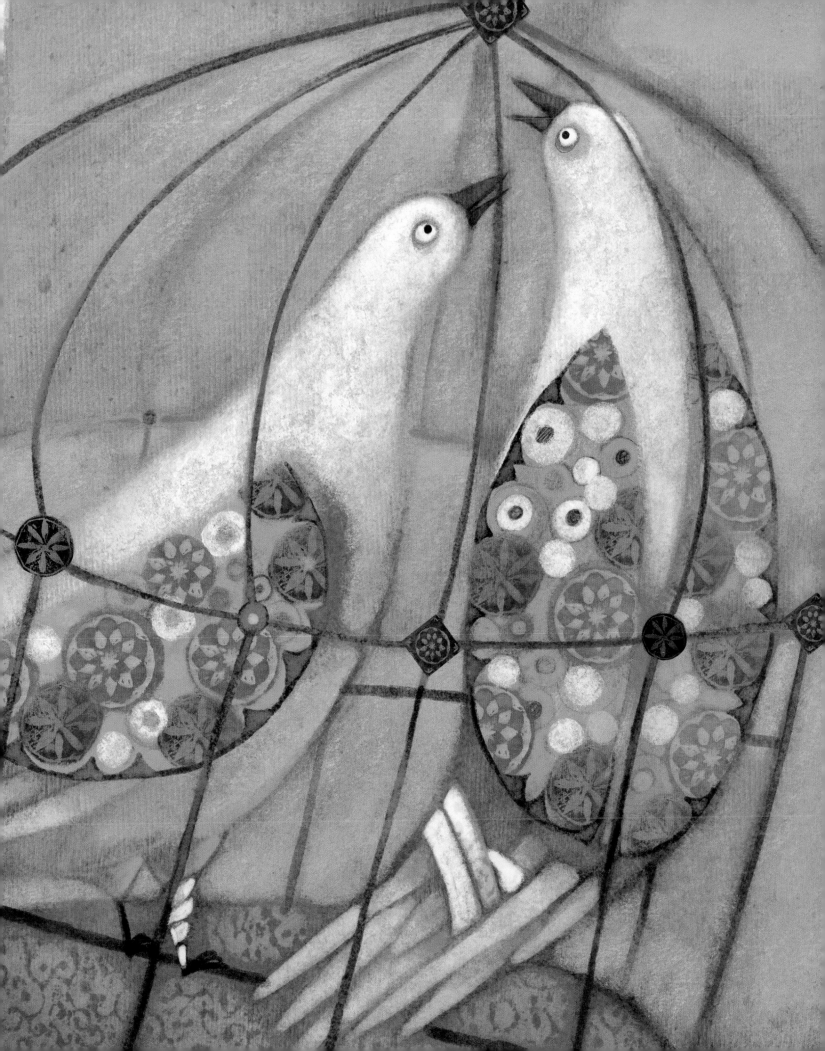

Mrs. Noah nursed the birds,
tended them, mended
their broken wings and legs.
She gave them water and food.
And they stared at her with their solemn eyes,
knowing that she would keep them safe
until they were well enough, or old enough,
to go off on their own.

Sometimes a freed bird came back to nest in a nearby tree.
Sometimes a freed bird came back to sing at Mrs. Noah's window.

But most often the birds did not return at all,
simply winging away into the great world.

But then the rains came.
Small drips as perfect as pearls.
Fat drops as big as ripe pears.
Drip, drop, drip, drop.

It rained and rained and rained
and did not stop.

Streams overflowed.
Rivers flooded.
Small towns drowned,
and large cities were threatened.

Mrs. Noah worried about the safety of her birds.
She moved the cages off the floor and onto a table.
She moved them from the table onto the stairs.
She wondered about the animals
out there in the flooded lands.
And she worried about her family.
She asked Mr. Noah for help.

Now, Mr. Noah loved his wife,
loved her generous heart.
"Do not worry," he said.
"God has told me what to do."
And in the morning,
with the help of his strong sons
and his strong daughters,
he began to build a boat.

It was designed to keep his family safe,
as well as animals—male and female of every kind.
(Or at least all the animals in the neighborhood.)
Plus Mrs. Noah's birds.
Two of each.
Eggs too.
She insisted.

Mr. Noah's boat was not small, of course.
It couldn't be with that many people and animals on board.
Not a rowboat or a dinghy.
Not a sailboat.
Not even a yacht.
It was a *huge* boat.
An ark.
A floating zoo,
with all the animals in cages
to keep them safe.
Just like Mrs. Noah's birds.

They sailed through big drops and
little drips,
through cloudbursts and gully washers.
They sailed for days, weeks, months . . .
until drip by drip, and drop by drop,
the rain stopped raining.

But could they see any dry land?
Not a meadow.
Not a field.
Not a town or city or farm.
Not even a mountain.
And that was the worrisome part.
Only water on every side.

So, Mrs. Noah sent out the birds
who were well enough to fly,
asking them to bring back proof
of some dry place where the ark might land.
She sent eagles to the east.

She sent ravens to the west.
But they did not come back.

She sent terns to the north.
And gulls to the south.
They did not come back.

At last she picked up her favorites,
a male and female dove
with their dusk-colored coats and soft manners.
"Go, my gray angels," she said,
releasing them into the air.
"Tell us if there is land."

Off the doves went, as a pair,
gray wing to gray wing.
They were gone one day.
Two days.
But on the third, they came back.
The male carried bits of grass in his beak.
The female brought back a twig
covered with red berries.

Above the ark appeared the largest rainbow
Mrs. Noah had ever seen.
At that, every creature great or small,
human or beast, bird or snake, celebrated.
And the doves began to build a nest.
Mrs. Noah smiled.
She knew that was a sign
that life on the earth was about to begin anew.